Michael Berenstain's
WHO AM I ?
A First Book of Famous People

A GOLDEN BOOK•NEW YORK

Western Publishing Company, Inc., Racine, Wisconsin 53404

Look—a brand-new penny!
Finding a penny means good luck.

This penny is so shiny that you can even
see Abraham Lincoln's bow tie on it.
    Why is Abraham Lincoln on the penny?
Why is he so famous?

And who are all these other
people on our money?
Who is this man wearing
a pigtail on the quarter?

4

I'm not really sure. But we can find out.
We can learn all about famous people right
here, in the Hall of Fame!

Wow! Look at all the pictures of
famous people.

Which one is Abraham Lincoln?

Here he is.

We can read about him on this label.

But let's not just read labels—let's have fun.

Let's pretend that we can go and visit Abraham Lincoln in person!

Abraham Lincoln
(1809–1865)

Abraham Lincoln was a great American president. His picture is on the five-dollar bill, as well as on the penny.

Lincoln was born and raised in a log cabin in the woods of Kentucky. As a young man, he was very tall and strong. He worked splitting fence rails and doing other farm chores.

Later, Lincoln studied hard and became
a lawyer. He was honest and fair. He was
famous for telling funny stories. People liked
him and called him "Honest Abe."

Lincoln ran for the office of president and
was elected.

While Lincoln was president, the Civil War began. It was a battle between Northern and Southern states over slavery.

Lincoln led the Northern states to victory, and the slaves were set free. But at the war's end, Lincoln was killed by a man who hated the North.

George Washington
(1732–1799)

Look! Here's the man wearing the pigtail on the quarter—George Washington. He was America's first president and a great soldier. His portrait is also on the one-dollar bill.

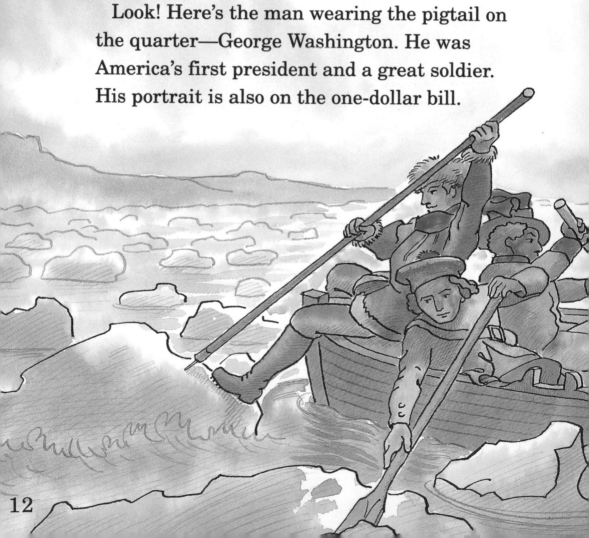

Washington led the American army during the Revolutionary War. The Americans fought the war to break free from England's rule.

Washington took his troops across the Delaware River on Christmas night and surprised the enemy while they were still celebrating. This victory helped America win the war.

Thomas Jefferson
(1743–1826)

Thomas Jefferson's portrait is on the nickel.
He was one of America's "Founding Fathers."
He was also America's third president.

Jefferson wrote the Declaration of Independence.
He finished in the hot, humid July of 1776.
It said that America was free from England.

That is why Americans celebrate Independence
Day every Fourth of July!

Franklin D. Roosevelt
(1882–1945)

Another great American president,
Franklin D. Roosevelt, appears on
the dime.

Roosevelt came from a wealthy
family. But he was famous for trying
to help poor people.

FDR

16

At the age of thirty-nine, Roosevelt was crippled by polio. He could only walk with crutches or a cane. In spite of this, he went on to become president.

He was president for twelve years—longer than anyone else.

Elizabeth II
(1926–   )

Other countries have famous people on their money, too.

Queen Elizabeth II's portrait is on all of England's coins. She became queen in 1952.

Another famous queen of England was Elizabeth I. Her navy defeated a great Spanish fleet that was sent to conquer England. That was the last time anyone tried to invade the British Isles.

**Elizabeth I
(1533–1603)**

Many of the most famous people in
history have been kings and queens.
One of the most famous of all was
Cleopatra—queen of ancient Egypt.

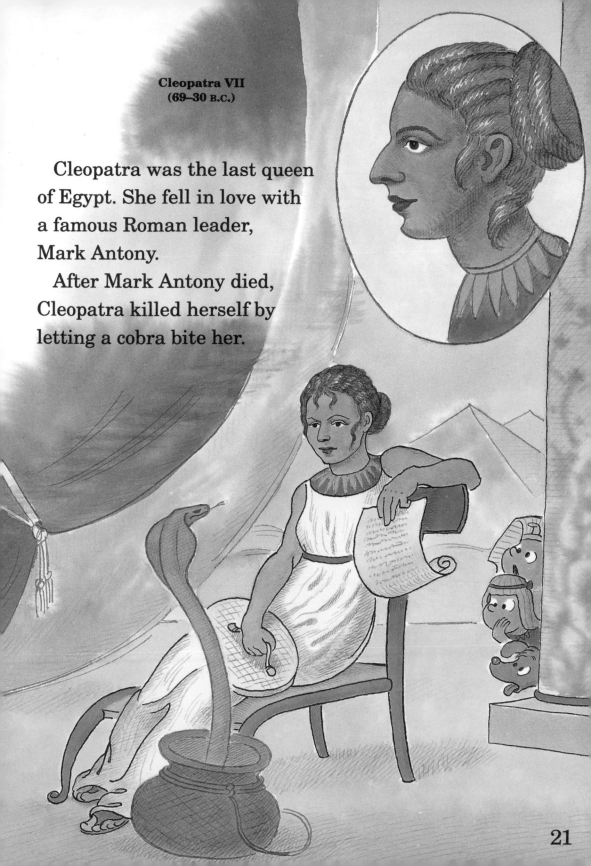

**Cleopatra VII
(69–30 B.C.)**

Cleopatra was the last queen
of Egypt. She fell in love with
a famous Roman leader,
Mark Antony.

After Mark Antony died,
Cleopatra killed herself by
letting a cobra bite her.

Can we find out about some famous people who didn't live so long ago?

John F. Kennedy was president of the United States from 1961 to 1963. As a young man, he commanded a torpedo boat in World War II.

Kennedy's boat was sunk by a Japanese destroyer. Though badly injured, Kennedy managed to get his crew to safety.

**John F. Kennedy
(1917–1963)**

Martin Luther King, Jr.
(1929–1968)

Another American leader of the 1960s was
Martin Luther King, Jr. He was a great man
of peace. King wanted black people in
America to be treated the same way as white
people. He led a great March on Washington
to demand rights for African-Americans.

Neil Armstrong
(1930-   )

Since the invention of the airplane, people
have become famous for flying higher, faster,
and farther than anyone before.

Neil Armstrong was the first person to walk
on the moon. In 1969 he and two other
American astronauts traveled 240,000 miles
from Earth to the moon in an *Apollo* spacecraft.

Amelia Earhart was a famous pilot in the early days of flying. She was the first woman to fly across the Atlantic Ocean. In 1935 she became the first person to fly alone from Hawaii to California.

**Amelia Earhart
(1897–1937)**

Leonardo da Vinci
(1452–1519)

Some people have become famous for doing many different things.

Leonardo da Vinci was a great artist. He painted the world's most famous picture, the *Mona Lisa*.

Leonardo da Vinci was also a great scientist and inventor. He drew some of the earliest designs for flying machines.

These machines were never built. Some, like the parachute and helicopter, would probably have worked quite well. Others, like the ornithopter, would not have flown. But it's fun to imagine what they would have been like.

parachute

helicopter

ornithopter
(bird-machine)

Many people have become famous for being great athletes.

Jesse Owens
(1913–1980)

Jesse Owens was one of the fastest runners in history. He won four gold medals in the 1936 Olympic Games.

Babe Ruth was a great baseball player. He began as a pitcher but became famous for his hitting. He hit sixty home runs in just one season!

**Babe Ruth
(1895–1948)**

Chris Evert was one of the best tennis players in recent history. She won her first big tournament when she was just sixteen years old.

**Chris Evert
(1954–   )**

Perhaps the most famous people of all are movie stars.

Judy Garland was the actress and singer who played Dorothy in *The Wizard of Oz*. Toto was played by a cairn terrier named Terry.

Judy Garland
(1922–1969)

Chico Marx
(1886–1961)

Groucho Marx
(1890–1977)

Harpo Marx
(1888–1964)

The Marx brothers—Chico, Groucho, and Harpo—were famous comedians. They have probably made more people laugh than anyone else in history. Their movies are as popular today as when they first appeared more than sixty years ago.

We've learned about some of the world's most
famous people.

Turn the page and see if you can remember
who they are.